A Righteous Cop

Published in the United States of America by Lulu.com

A Righteous Cop

I'll never forget the first time I killed a man.

Wait...I'm getting way ahead of myself calling it a killing. Yes, I did kill him, but you couldn't really classify it as a murder. I shot him in order to save an innocent person's life, in the line of duty.

I used to be a cop.

Well, I'm still a cop, but I guess I just don't feel like one. A righteous cop, anyway.

I almost lost everything.

#

It was a justified shooting – a young man by the name of Tommy Ray Wallace.

To say that Tommy was born on the wrong side of the tracks was putting it mildly.

Born to an alcoholic mother and a father with a violent criminal background, Tommy had quickly become the poster boy for a dysfunctional family and child abuse.

By the time he was fifteen-years-old, he had already spent six months in a juvenile detention center for vandalism, theft, and killing a neighbor's dog with a baseball bat. Upon his release, the first thing he'd done was shoplift a bottle of liquor and gone on another violent rampage, this time attacking the liquor store's owner, choking him into unconsciousness.

And he was just getting started.

#

His short, pathetic life came full circle at the age of seventeen, when, upon returning to his parent's home to retrieve some of his clothing, walked in on his mother having an affair with a strange man and had proceeded to beat him within an inch of his life.

The man survived – barely – and, in fear for his life, had declined to press charges against Tommy. His mother, though, was a different story altogether. Feigning concern for her only son's welfare and that of the general public, she did press charges against him, and he was sent back to the detention center again, and after his eighteenth birthday, was transferred to a prison for the remainder of his five year sentence.

Due to prison overcrowding, he was paroled after serving only three years of his original sentence, and upon his release, went straight back to his parent's home and proceeded to kill both of them with his father's own handgun.

Then he was in the wind.

That's when we met – for the first and last time.

#

I had been patrolling the East end of Bloomington, Indiana – known fondly by local, law-abiding residents as "the Wild East End" - a community of dilapidated trailer parks, ancient, abandoned homes that had been turned into meth labs, two liquor stores, and a pool hall – slash – bar and grill that mainly catered to drug dealers, rednecks, alcoholics, and lonely hearts looking for love in all the wrong places.

I was sitting at a stoplight, lighting a cigarette and rolling my window down when the call came through about Tommy.

Having no prior, first-hand knowledge of Tommy or his pathetic past, I shifted the cruiser into high gear and headed toward the East end only a few blocks away. Big tough guy cop who loves old Clint Eastwood Dirty Harry flicks headed toward his destiny and all that good shit.

I had absolutely *no* idea of what awaited me once I got there.

Then again, Tommy had no idea it was going to be his last day on Earth, either.

When I pulled into the liquor store parking lot, there was Tommy, standing there holding a young woman by throat with one hand and using his free hand to press the blade of a large hunting knife against her carotid artery. The fear in her eyes was so *real*, nothing like you see in the movies. No Hollywood actress could ever pull this look off as well as a *real* victim of violent crime.

One of the first things I noticed as I jumped out of the cruiser was the absence of anyone else in the parking lot but me, Tommy, and the young woman he was holding captive. No other customers, no other cops, *nobody*. It was as though time had stood still for us, everything moving in slow motion, like the three of us were caught up in some kind of time warp.

And the only way out was going to be to shoot Tommy.

He had a wild, crazy, I'll-go-down-dead-before-you-take-me sort of look in his eyes, and the woman was screaming at the top of her lungs, a deafening, high-pitched, piss-your-pants type of scream that would have put any B-horror film actress to shame.

I already had my service weapon pulled and was poised in the standard defensive position, my shoulders squared, my feet about shoulder length apart, my Glock aimed right at his forehead. I couldn't get a good heart shot, with the woman blocking my view.

"Drop the knife and let the girl go, asshole!" I screamed, doing my best bad-ass cop impression. You had to let them know you meant business, and you wouldn't think twice about blowing their brains out. If you let them see fear in *your* eyes, they would play on that, have the upper hand. You had to be just as crazy – if not more crazy – than they are.

He didn't even bat an eye. He had the wild eyes going on, but otherwise spoke very calmly, as though my threatening his life hadn't fazed him a bit. He was actually grinning. He said, "I don't think so, asshole. Drop that gun or I'll cut this bitch's head off." He pressed the blade against her throat just hard enough to draw a bead of blood, and upon feeling the blood streaming down her neck, she woman began screaming even louder now, losing her mind.

I stepped two feet closer, for a better head shot. I said, in the most stern, authoritative tone I could muster, "I said, drop the knife, or I'll be forced to shoot you. Last chance."

His response was to press the blade even harder against her throat, drawing even more blood, and she flew into a blind panic then, screaming and squirming to get free of his grip, endangering her own life even further.

That's when I took the shot.

My aim was true. The bullet struck Tommy right between the eyes, sending him sprawling backward, the girl falling with him, landing right on top of him. She immediately began scampering away from him, on her hands and knees, still screaming like a banshee. I ran to her and tried to calm her down her but she was too far gone by then to hear anything I said.

She never thanked me for saving her life, either. Imagine that.

#

Yet...I couldn't get the shooting out of my mind. Had trouble finding any real justification for his death at my hands. They say some cops can handle the guilt and some can't. I guess I could be classified in the latter category.

The memory of that day was always with me. It hung over me like a death shroud, a constant cloud cover that was always blocking out the sun. Even on the most beautiful day I would feel dark and dreary and deeply depressed – and, at one point, even suicidal.

My wife was the first to notice my mood swings and overall change in my daily routine. My personal hygiene began to suffer, and my eating habits and sleeping habits changed dramatically over a very short period of time. Thank God my kids were still too young at the time to pick up on it. Or maybe they had picked up on it, but were patient with me in hopes that someday they would no longer have to watch their father fall apart before their eyes.

Then, in the midst of all my personal pain and

turmoil, I was at the liquor store one day – the same liquor store where I'd taken Tommy's life in the parking lot – and lo and behold, there was his grandmother, Pearl, perched on an old lawn chair in the side lot, staring holes through me as I exited the store with a carton of cigarettes.

I'd seen her picture in the newspaper way back when the details of the shooting had made the front page. ***Courageous Cop Saves Woman's Life***, the headline had read. ***Local Career Criminal's Reign of terror Comes To An End***, read another.

And right below the article, a picture of Tommy's grandmother, her eyes wet with tears, telling *her* side of the story, about how some rookie cop trying to make a name for himself had shot her grandson in cold blood.

The second I saw her I made it a point to look away and make a mad dash for my used Chevy Malibu with worn out tires and expired plates when, undeterred by my attempt to avoid her, she said, "You...you're the one who shot my grandson."

Instead of jumping into my car and hightailing it out of the lot, for some reason, call it guilt or morbid curiosity or a glutton for punishment or what-not, I stopped dead in my tracks, and turned to face her down.

Swallowing the lump in my throat, I said, "Excuse me?"

She squirmed around in the lawn chair, lit a Pall Mall non-filter, and said, "I said, you're the one who shot my grandson. I recognized you, alright." She dragged off her cigarette and continued. "You look...*different*, now. Don't look so good. I always heard a guilty conscience will do that to a man."

Lighting a cigarette myself, I replied, "It was a

justified shooting. He would have killed that girl...I could see it in his eyes."

Flipping her cigarette into the bushes nearby, she retorted, "That what they call it now? Justified? He had a knife, you had a gun. Wasn't no contest there. Besides, I know – *knew* – my grandson. He was just blowing smoke up your ass, acting all tough. He wouldn't have *really* killed that girl. He just wanted you to *think* he would have."

I said, without thought or hesitation, "Well, he should have thought about that before he got drunk and crazy and took a hostage, huh?"

Lighting another cigarette, she said, "It was me that had to identify the body, his mama wasn't around to do it. You know why he shot her, his own mama?"

I had a very good idea why Tommy had thought shooting his own mother was justified, but out of curiosity as to why his grandmother thought so, I said, "No, enlighten me."

She said, "You didn't read his record? That's hard to believe. Anyway, I was all he had left except for Danny, and I could only do so much, in my condition. Ever hear of COPD, Mr tough guy?"

I said, "So...you think chain smoking is going to help your condition?"

"Better than my grandson's current condition, ain't it?" she said. "You ever smelled a dead body, Mr hero?"

I had, more than once. There's no other smell like it. You could often tell just how long someone had been dead just by the stench. Imagine a pound of rancid, rotting hamburger. Then *multiply* that by *each* pound, say up to one-hundred and fifty to two-hundred pounds. Then add in some maggots, flies, body gases, and seeping body fluids. And often times, upon death, a person's bladder and bowels let go at the time of death, adding even more rancid odor to the mix. Oh yes...there is no other smell like it in the world.

Feeling a little queasy, I said, "Yes, of course. I'm a cop." As good an answer as any, I'd thought, under the circumstances.

She lit another cigarette and said, "That's the way my grandson smelled, when I went to ID the body. Damn coroner's meat locker broke down. Can you imagine that? His grand-mama standing there, smelling that awful smell and looking at the big hole in his head?"

No, I thought, glumly. *I couldn't imagine having to ID one of my own kids or grandkids and having to smell that.* But what I said was, "I'm sorry, lady, really I am. But like I said, it *was* a justified shooting, and I saved someone's life in the process. It was, what I refer to as, a win- win situation, in the end."

She flipped her cigarette into the bushes again and said, "You just keep on thinking that, Mr hero. You keep on fooling yourself into thinking it was a righteous kill. Keep on thinking that each and *every* time you pop open another bottle just to keep your head on straight. Besides, just like my grandson, you'll pay for your sins soon enough, too. Difference is, you will be a miserable, shitty mess of a man by your *own* hand, where my Tommy boy never stood a chance in hell from the time he was born." She lit another cigarette. "You just *think* about that."

As I turned to walk back to my car, I thought, *Oh, don't worry, lady. I already do, and I imagine I will until the day I die. But sure, why not add a little more insult to injury, right? I'm already a walking corpse.*

And I can see my obituary now: *Ben Striker, local hero cop, found dead from guilt and lung cancer.* Now, there is an epitaph for my kids to be proud of.

#

Actually, I am very lucky I didn't end up being just like Tommy Ray Wallace. My father was the kind of guy you'd picture as a model for an old Norman Rockwell painting, a guy sitting on a porch in an old rocking chair, smoking a corn cob pipe and reading a copy of *National Geographic* or *Arizona Highways*.

But you wouldn't see a faithful old hound dog lying next to the rocking chair, because my father *hated* pets around the house. It had taken me three months to talk him into letting me have a goldfish, and even then he complained about the fish shit odor coming from the tank. But I guess when you slammed down about a case of Pabst Blue Ribbon a day and had the demeanor of an angry pit bull you could always find something to complain about.

But my memories of my Father are the least of my worries these days.

#

Each morning when I look in my bathroom mirror, it is *Tommy's* face I see, staring back at me accusingly, a ghostly reflection that seems to float right through the misty glass and permeates my very soul.

The only thing that prevents me from cutting my throat is my curiosity about the fragments of memory that bubble to the surface of my mind like turds in a sewer. Some good, some bad. But mostly bad.

That and my family; if it weren't for them, I'd surely have given up by now.

But for now, I'm going to grab a pack of cigarettes, a glass of sun tea, and retire to the back patio and watch the sun go down with my wife, while our beautiful daughters play Frisbee nearby, totally oblivious to my current psychological condition.

Ah...the naive happiness of a child before it is so cruelly ripped away.

Just like the night in the liquor store parking lot, when mine was ripped away as well. I wish my children the best of luck in this world; they are going to need it.

For now, I light a cigarette and sip my tea, as my mind tells me, *It was a righteous kill.*

But my heart screams *murderer.*

Will my heart and mind ever stop pulling me in so many different directions? Maybe, maybe not.

As if my wife can read my mind, she reaches over and grasps my hand gently in her own, gives it a little squeeze, winks at me, and whispers *I love you.*

For now, that's all I really need.

#

Or so I'd thought.

As time went on, and more days turned into weeks and the weeks turned into months, I wasn't really sure what I'd needed to feel *normal* again.

The world is full of broken people, lonely people, hungry people.

It's part of the natural order of things. But, splints, casts, so called miracle drugs, or even time itself, can't mend broken hearts, wounded minds, or spirits torn asunder.

As Charle Chaplin once said, "In the end, everything is just a gag." He apparently was an optimist by nature. Me?

Not so. I'd always had alot of trouble finding a silver lining in every cloud, or a pot of gold at the end of every rainbow. In other words, I may have *read* fiction, or *watched* it on the screen, but, I didn't *live it.* I tried my best to remain in a virtual state of reality, no matter how hard times were to deal with.

The reality of my situation was, I was slowly but surely spiraling down into a deep, dark, place I wouldn't be able to dig myself out of.

#

My wife was the first person to notice the change.

She had actually noticed the change in me long before I thought she had, but had kept it to herself in hopes that I would come out of it on my own, but it hadn't taken her long to see that wasn't going to happen.

Still, she kept her feelings to herself, to not enrage me further, not that I would have hurt my family, of course. I was my own worst enemy, as far as anything physical was concerned.

Still, I couldn't blame her for her silence. A man like myself, in that state of mind, I'd imagine could be very intimidating and frightening without necessarily trying to be.

Then came the drinking.

I'd never really been a heavy drinker.

I mean, sure, when I was a kid, hanging out with my equally goofy friends, I'd taken part in some binge drinking, hitting the keg parties, etc. But it hadn't taken me very long to realize that alcoholism wasn't going to be part of my daily agenda.

That is, until I met up with Tommy Ray Wallace, and my life changed forever.

#

I remember the first time my wife had mentioned that she'd noticed my problem.

I guess it was hard to miss, smoking about three packs a day and consuming more than a fifth of vodka each day without fail.

I'd been sitting out back on the patio, watching the neighbor's dog running through the sprinklers, when the sound of Veronica's voice snapped me back into reality.

"Ben? Earth to Ben, come in please."

Her attempt at sarcasm wasn't totally lost on me, as I forced a smile and said, "Earth to Veronica. I hear you loud and clear."

She stood right in front of me then, with her hands on her hips like a drill Sergeant, and said, "That's really funny, Ben. Are you gomg to eat dinner or not?"

I looked out at the oncoming sunset to realize I'd been sitting out there for hours, sipping and smoking and sipping some more, until I'd lost all track of time – and reality.

I said, "What's for dinner?"

She said, "Like I told you several times already, I ordered pizza and bread sticks for the girls, and baked spaghetti for us. That was two hours ago, of course, so I'll have to warm it up for you, that is, if you're even still interested."

I said, "Sure, I'll be ready in just a minute."

She said, "You said that two hours ago, too."

The vodka, having made me impatient and rude, prompted me to say, "I *said*, I'll be there in a *minute*."

"Fine," she said, and turned to walk away. When she reached the patio doors, she said, "Oh, and you pissed yourself again."

I looked down at my lap to see she was right; sometime, over the last few hours, my body had been so numb from the alcohol, I hadn't even felt it when I soiled my pants.

#

That was the first time Veronica had begun to notice my problem, except for the obvious, that is.

It's almost impossible not to notice that your husband of twenty five years can no longer control his bladder or bowels.

It doesn't take a rocket scientist to figure out that your spouse should be wearing adult diapers – and *why* he should be.

But leave it to me to not even notice.

Then again, you would have to *sober* long enough to know when you needed to void your bladder, too.

One night, as I sat at the kitchen table eating some of Veronica's famous chili, she said, "Is it good?"

I said, "Of course, as always."

She said, "Well, it's good to see you eating instead of drinking."

I said, "May I please just eat my dinner in peace?"

She said, "Sure, sorry babe."

I went back to eating just as my two girls, Holly and Jean walked in, and Holly said, "Daddy, can I ask you something?"

I said, "Sure, sugar pie. What's up?"

She said, sadly, "Are you okay?"

I said, "I'm fine, honey. I'm just taking a vacation from work so I can feel better, that's all." *A lie.*

Jean said, "Some girls at school today were social networking, and one of the posts said you didn't have to shoot that guy, but you did it anyway."

I said, "If I hadn't shot him, he would have killed his hostage. That woman would be dead."

Veronica said, "That's right, girls. Your dad is a *hero*, not a bad guy. He saved someone's life that day. I want you to always remember that."

Holly smiled and said, "Cool!" Then the both of them toddled off into the living room to watch TV. Veronica said, "You really *are* a hero, Ben. I wish you'd realize that."

I said, "I know I was justified, but for some reason, I still harbor such a strong feeling of guilt. I don't understand."

She said, "Maybe you should see a counselor?"

I said, "You mean a shrink, don't you? Some little guy who looks just like Sigmund Freud and picks at my brain? No thanks."

She said, "I know you don't like the idea, but I think it would really help you."

I said, adamantly, "*No*, Veronica. The answer is a resounding *no*."

She stood up from the table, pushed her bowl of

half eaten chili into the floor, and stormed out of the room, mumbling under her breath. I couldn't blame her, but at the same time, I felt angry toward her was well, like she'd betrayed me when I'd needed her the most.

What I didn't understand at the time was, I was betraying myself – and my family.

#

The next morning, I'd woke up with one of those hangovers from hell, my head pounding and my eyes half blind and my guts tied up in knots.

I'd waited until the girls had climbed on the school bus and Veronica has left for work at the hospital and took a quick shower and took a drive down to the neighborhood package store for another bottle of vodka.

My liquid salvation.

The only thing that *really* understood me at the time.

Or so I'd thought.

Upon walking out of the package store, I glanced up to see no other than Tommy's grandmother, Pearl, perched on an old lawn chair in the side lot again, staring holes through me as I exited the store with my bottle.

She said, "So, I see you are *drinking* your breakfast again today. A guilty consience will do that to a man. Tear him right down."

I said, "I don't feel guilty about a damn thing."

She grinned and said, "Sure you don't. That's why you are slowly but surely losing your whole life to the bottle, but your fuddled mind tells you something different. That's why it's called the *demon* alcohol."

I said, "I call it relaxing."

She said, "Yeah, well, if you get too much more relaxed, you'll be in a coma."

I popped the cap on the bottle, took a big sip, placed the cap back on, and said, "There, that's better."

She said, "For now, maybe. But not for long, Mister righteous cop."

I said, "Meaning?"

She said, "Soon enough, you'll understand. You see, a real, dedicated, drunk starts off being a regular guy walking through a sick world trying not to get shit on his shoes. So he drinks a little. Then he drinks a lot. He loses his job first, then his family. And then his house. And the whole time, suffering from that guilt, that eats away at his guts like cancer. Then one day, he just blows his *own* brains out, and does everybody a favor."

Taking another sip from the bottle, I placed the cap back on and said, "I don't intend to give you that pleasure, Mrs Wallace. Is there anything else you have to say? I have things to do."

She stood up, spit on the ground at my feet, and said, "Just one more thing."

As I turned to leave, I said, "Which is?"

She said, "Just remember, that guilt you carry around with you? It'll kill you a lot quicker than that bottle ever will."

#

On the way home, I couldn't help but think about what the department shrink had told me on the phone a few weeks ago.

He had said, *A man keeps drinking like this, sooner or later, he is a broken toilet of a man who is living in a cardboard box and drinking cheap wine out of a paper bag with money he begged from strangers on the street.*

But I didn't see myself that way.

Not *yet*, anyway.

So I drove on.

I wasn't in the mood to sit around the house by myself that day, so I decided to take a country cruise instead, away from the hustle and bustle of the city and the low life criminals within, just waiting to try my patience once again.

Make me *shoot* them.

So I drove on down the quiet country roads, with my radio blaring, sipping my bottle and day dreaming about the way things used to be, when I was a kid, when you didn't have to worry about criminals ruling the streets.

I was happy again – that is, until I realized I lost track of time, and it was late afternoon already.

Close to dinner time.

As I turned around to head toward home before Veronica got off work, I was suddenly overcome by the urge to drop by my old Church, the First Baptist, and pay a visit to Pastor Jim Whitsell.

I knew he could give me some good advice.

#

As I walked into the Church, there was Pastor Jim, dusting off the podium and whistling to himself. I couldn't help but think how unhappy he might be after I told him what I intended to discuss with him.

He turned to see me, gave me a big smile and a wave, and said, "Well, hello, Ben. Long time, no see."

I sat down in one of the front pews and said, "I know, Jim. Sorry I haven't been to a service in a while. I've had a lot on my mind."

Jim sat down next to me and said, "All the more reason to attend a service. So, what's on your mind, Ben?"

I said, "If I tell you, I'm afraid you might consider me a very bad man."

Jim said, "No man is so bad, that he can't be forgiven in the eyes of God, Ben. Go on, and tell me what's on your mind."

I said, "I suppose, by now, you've heard about the shooting of Tommy Wallace."

Jim said, "Yes, Ben. It was a terrible thing. He had such a pitiful upbringing."

I said, "Yes, his grandmother made sure to tell me all about it."

Jim said, "Are you feeling guilty about it, Ben?"

I said, "I had been, until today. Now, when I look back on that day, I feel *glad* that I shot him."

Jim said, "Oh my, that isn't a good thing."

I said, "I'm not done with the story yet. After I shot him? I realized that I *enjoyed* shooting him."

Jim shook his head and said, "Oh my, Ben. That doesn't sound like you at all."

I said, "Normally, it wouldn't be like me to enjoy

seeing another person suffer. But that day, when he was standing there holding a knife to that woman's throat, I *hated* him. Hated a total stranger, and *wanted* to end his life."

Jim said, "Ben, you took his life to *save* the life of an innocent person. That, I think God would understand. But your lingering feelings of hatred, not so much. You need to ask for forgiveness, redeem yourself, and do it now."

Standing to my feet, I said, "And I don't choose to do so? Will I fall from grace with God?"

Jim said, "I don't know what to say, Ben. I'm having very conflicted feelings about this now, too."

I said, "You and me both, Pastor. You and me both."

Then I turned to leave. Jim called after me, trying to stop me from leaving, but I paid him no mind.

#

I pulled up in the driveway to see Veronica had beat me home. I took a quick sip from the bottle, stashed it under th front seat, climbed out, locked the door behind me, and went inside.

Veronica was sitting at the table sipping coffee and reading the newspaper. She said, "Well, where have you been?"

I said, "I just took a drive in the country, to clear my head."

She said, "Did it work?"

Sitting down at the table, I said, "I guess I'll know soon enough. Where are the girls?"

She said, "It's Friday night, and they wanted to

know if they could spend the night over at Lisa's house. You know, their friend who is a cheerleader."

I said, "Well, I hope they have fun."

She said, "Speaking of which, what shall we do now that we have a night to ourselves?"

I said, "How about dinner at a restaurant?"

She said, "What? No takeout pizza or chili? Are you feeling alright?"

I forced a smile and said, "I'm okay. I just thought we could spend an evening doing something other than me sitting on the patio drowning my sorrows, that's all."

Her face lit up and she said, "Well, let's go, before you change your mind."

#

I let her pick the restaurant, and we ate at a combo bar and grill that supposedly served up some really good butterfly shrimp.

As we sat nibbling on the appetizers – bread sticks and some very tasty dipping sauce – she said, "Well, is this place satisfactory?"

I said, "Oh yes, it's fine. But these bread sticks are making me mighty thirsty."

She said, "I want some iced tea. How about you?"

I said, "I was thinking of a good red wine to go with our shrimp. Do you mind?"

Studying my face for a moment, she said, "Are you sure that's a good idea?"

I said, "What's wrong with some red wine? It's supposed to be good with sea food."

She said, "You know what I mean, Ben."

I said, "It's *glass* of wine, not a *gallon* of wine."

She said, "One glass?"

I said, "Just forget it."

She said, "Don't be upset, babe, okay? I was just looking after your best interests."

Tossing my napkin on the floor, I said, "And I don't need a babysitter to monitor my diet."

She sighed, stood up, and said, "And I don't need to sit here and watch my husband make a drunken fool of himself, so I guess we're at an impasse."

Standing up, I said, "Then I guess our dinner date is *over.*"

Her eyes wet with tears, she said, "Then I guess it is." Then she turned and walked away, toward the front doors, and was gone into the night. As I made my way to the register to pay for a dinner that never took place, I could just *feel* the eyes of the other patrons staring at me, like I was an asshole.

By the time I'd walked outside, Veronica was nowhere in sight.

#

I'd found her about two blocks away, stomping down the sidewalk in her heels.

I pulled up beside her, rolled down my window, and said, "Come on, Veronica. Get in."

She stopped, took off her heels, tossed them at me, and said, "I'll walk if it's okay with you."

I said, "Please, babe. Just get in. I don't want you walking home in the dark, alone."

She said, "Then you shouldn't have acted like such an *ass* during our so called dinner date."

I said, "Okay, I'm *sorry.* Please, get in, okay?"

She stood glaring at me for a moment, lit a cigarette, and said, "Okay, but I'm doing so under protest."

I said, "Duly noted. Now, get in – please, with sugar on top."

She climbed into the *back* seat for the ride home.

#

Once we pulled into the driveway, she was out of the back seat and slamming the car door behind her and stomping through the front door before I could even open the driver's door.

She was *not* a happy camper.

Then again, neither was I.

By the time I had come through the front door, she was already sitting at the kitchen table, smoking a cigarette and drumming her fingertips on the table top.

I walked in, stood leaning against the far wall, and said, "Are you calmed down yet?"

She just shook her head, and said, "About as calm as I'm liable to be for now."

I said, "Then I should just buzz off, then?"

She said, "That's up to you."

I said, "I think I need some fresh air."

She said, "Then you should go outside and leave me alone."

I didn't say another word; I just walked back out the front door, opened the driver's side door of the Chevy, retrieved my bottle, and took a big sip.

Then another.

That's when I saw him, whoever he was.

As I lowered the bottle to get a better look, I could

see an old, beat up Ford pickup truck, green in color, parked directly across the street from our driveway. In the driver's seat sat a man that looked vaguely familiar, but I knew it couldn't be him, because he was *dead.*

Maybe a relative? I thought, nervously. *It's very possible.*

A relative of Tommy Wallace.

A brother, maybe? Or an Uncle?

I guess I'd find out soon enough.

As I stood staring at him, taking another sip from the bottle, he just smiled, flipped me the middle finger, and drove away into the night in a cloud of black smoke, the old Ford having seen it's better days.

Then he was gone.

But I knew deep down in my heart he'd be back soon enough.

#

As I sat on the patio, mulling over just how I was going to tell Veronica about our mystery guest in the Ford truck, I heard the patio doors slide open, and within a few seconds, there she was, standing right in front of me, shaking her head in disbelief.

She said, "So, I see you are drowning your sorrows as usual, instead of facing up to your problems."

I said, "I'm more than a little nervous right now."

She said, "You mean, you're more than a little hungover right now, don't you?"

I said, "We need to talk, Veronica."

She said, "Well, no shit, Ben."

I said, "Not about my drinking, either. We have a

much bigger problem right now."

She sat down next to me and said, "And just what could be more important than your own problem?"

I said, "There is something I haven't told you about. *Someone* I haven't told you about."

She rolled her eyes and said, "Dear God. *Please* don't tell me you're having an affair."

I said, "No, I'm *not* having an affair. I'm being followed by someone."

She looked genuinely confused and said, "What in the hell are you talking about, Ben?"

I said, "I have been "approached" by Tommy Wallace's grandmother twice now, and tonight, I'm pretty damn sure that one of his male relatives was parked across the street from our house."

She said, "My God, Ben. What have you gotten us into?"

I said, "Would you rather me not have saved that woman's life?"

She said, "To be honest, Ben? I'm not sure what I think you should have done now. I know that sounds awful to say, but your actions have intruded on *our* lives now, and the lives of our children."

I said, "That's why as of now, I want you and the girls to pack up and go stay at your mother's place. She'd be thrilled to have you and the girls there, too."

She said, "That's fine, but just what am I supposed to tell our girls, Ben? First you kill someone, then you turn into a drunk, and now, some homicidal maniac is going to run us out of our own home? Where is it going to end, Ben?"

I said, "It ends when I say it ends."

She said, "What does that mean?"

I said, "Just go pack and I'll take care of the rest."

She walked away without saying another word, her eyes filled with tears.

After she was out of earhshot, I cried like a baby until I couldn't cry anymore.

#

After Veronica had driven over to Lisa's house to pick up the girls, I had made a call to the precinct to talk with the Chief of police, Harlan Crow.

I dreaded to hear what he'd have to say about my situation, after he'd already suspended me, but I felt I had no choice under the circumstances.

He answered on the third ring, with a tone in his voice like someone who has just poured their nightcap to help them sleep, and wasn't very happy about being bothered.

He said, "Yeah? This better be good."

I said, "Chief, it's Ben Striker."

Crow said, "Then this better be *real* good."

I said, "I have a big problem."

Crow said, "I know that already, Striker. Can you be more specific?"

I said, "My current problem has to do with the Wallace family."

Crow said, "As in Tommy Ray Wallace?"

I said, "Yes."

Crow said, "Then you *do* have a problem. What, exactly, are they doing to cause you concern?"

I said, "First of all, his grandmother won't leave me alone. Now, one of his other relatives is parking across the street from my place after dark."

Crow said, "Have they threatened you or your family? Made death threats?"

I said, "No, not directly."

Crow said, "Have they destroyed any property or trespassed?"

I said, glumly, "No, not yet."

Crow said, "Then I can't do anything, not legally, that is."

I said, "I know that. I just wanted to give you a heads-up, and ask you for a small favor."

Crow said, "Which is?"

I said, "Could you have an extra patrol car cruise by Veronica's mother's house for now? I told her to take the girls over there for the time being."

Crow said, "Will do. And Ben?"

I said, "Yes, sir?"

Crow said, "Lay low, and *sober up*. That is, if you still want to be a cop."

I said, "Will do," and hung up.

But I wasn't sure if I could keep my word or not.

#

After talking to Crow, I called my mother in law's house. She answered, and said, abruptly, "Yes, Ben?"

I said, "Verna, are Veronica and the girls there yet?"

She said, "Yes, but they are trying to rest right now."

I said, "Okay. Could you relay a message for me, then?"

She said, "I guess so."

I said, "Fine. Just tell her and the girls I love

them, and I will be in touch soon."

She said, "Whatever."

Then she hung up.

A few minutes later, I was sipping from the bottle again.

#

About an hour later, I was sitting on the patio, crying like a baby again.

But at least I was *alone* now, my family now safe from my latest binge of alcohol and self pity.

But I, myself, was far from safe and secure. I was now a walking, breathing, human *target*, the object of a vengeful, violent, criminal family that would seemingly stop at nothing to exact their revenge against me for taking Tommy's life.

First, they would torment me psychologically, then, after they were done ruining my mind, they would come after me physically.

I tried to banish the thought from my mind, by breaking open a fresh bottle.

It didn't work.

#

After a long hot shower, I went to bed.

I didn't sleep much, though.

My mind kept racing and my heart was pounding at the thought of *that* day.

The day I pulled the trigger on Tommy Wallace.

The day my life – and my family's lives – changed forever.

#

I climbed out of bed around dawn.

After slipping on my bathrobe and pouring myself some fortified coffee, I slipped my .357 magnum I kept for protection into the pocket of my robe, and walked out on the patio.

What I saw made my blood run cold.

Sitting in my lawn chair was no other than the man I'd seen parked across the street the night before.

I stopped dead in my tracks, slipping my right hand into the pocket of my robe, and cocking the hammer back on the .357.

He was facing me, sitting in the chair with his legs crossed, smoking a cigarette and grinning like something was funny. I didn't see the humor in it at all. I said, "And you are?"

The man said, "So, is that a gun you have in there, or are you just glad to see me?"

I said, "I don't find anything about this situation funny."

He said, "Myself? I think this whole thing is *hilarious*, for you to think you're safe just because you have a gun."

I said, "Most people tend to think they're safe on their own property, and with a loaded weapon. But since you apparently have no common sense, I guess you wouldn't see it that way."

The man said, "I got enough common sense to know a man who is scared shitless when I see one."

I said, "You mean the gun? I don't really need it. It

just heightens my sense of security."

The man grinned and said, "Fair enough. But, just remember, mister tough guy cop, if you point a gun at a man, you best be willing to shoot him."

I stepped forward, pulled out the .357, and said, "Like I shot your brother?"

The man took a deep breath, exhaled, and said, "Don't you mean how you *murdered* my brother?"

I said "Your brother had a knife to a woman's throat. I had no other choice."

The man said, "Yes you did. You could have talked him down."

I said, "I don't make a habit of trying to talk sense to a homicidal maniac holding a knife to someone's carotid artery. Now, I think you better leave."

The man stood up, flipped his cigarette on the ground, and said, "Or what?"

I raised the .357, pointed it right at his face, and said, "Or I'll blow your head off."

The man could apparently see it in my eyes, I wasn't bluffing. He said, "I have things to do, anyway. But I will be back, you can count on it."

I said, "I can't wait."

Then the man – supposedly Tommy's brother – turned and left without another word. Moments later, I could hear the old Ford sputtering to life somewhere close by, and after a few seconds, I didn't hear it any longer.

Then I lowered my gun, sat down in my lawn chair, and got sick to my stomach.

I had almost killed another man in less than a few weeks.

I went back inside, washed down two sleeping

pills with some vodka, and went back to bed.

I didn't wake up again until my cell phone rang that afternoon.

#

It was Chief Crow, checking in on me.

As I fumbled with the phone I heard him say, "So, I hear you had a visitor."

Yawning, I said, "How did you know?"

He said, "One of our patrol officers was driving by, said he saw that old Ford sputtering down the street close to your place. He isn't very obvious, is he?"

Lighting a cigarette, I said, "He's an idiot."

Crow said, "You *think*?"

I said, "I *know* he is."

Crow said, "So, is everything okay otherwise? You taking care of yourself, keeping your shit wired tight?"

I said, "As best I can, yes." *Another lie.*

Crow said, "Good, keep it that way."

I said, "Is there anything else you want to tell me? I need to wake up and eat dinner."

Crow said, "Nope, except I still have extra patrols on your mother in law's house. So far, no suspicious activity."

Breathing a sigh of relief, I said, "Well, that's a good thing."

Crow said, "We'll talk soon." Then he hung up.

I hung up, climbed out of bed, and tried to choke down a TV dinner.

It didn't work out.

#

Two hours later, I was sitting on the patio, watching the sun go down, and sipping vodka on the rocks.

Sunsets in Indiana were something we'd grown to love. The way everything turned to a blinding gold and shined as if it were the only place on the earth. As if the sunset was meant for us alone.

For Veronica and I.

Now here I was alone, watching the sunset by myself, sipping vodka and missing my wife so much it physically hurt me on the inside, in my heart.

I missed my girls, too.

I couldn't help but wonder what Holly and Jean were thinking about me now; killer, or hero?

I poured another drink.

#

And another.

I don't remember much after that.

#

The next morning, after a long hot shower and a six pack of beer, I was ready to face the world.

At least temporarily.

I'd been giving a lot of thought to my current dilemma – the very uncomfortable situation with the Wallace family – and I'd decided to pay a visit to Tommy Wallace's grave.

Not out of guilt, mind you, but out of respect. I was, after all, the man who took his life – even if it was in the line of duty.

It was around noon when I arrived at the cemetery office. The lady working the desk had directed me to the Wallace plot, but had informed me that he didn't have a gravestone yet; the family couldn't afford one.

Upon finding the plot, I could see it was nothing more than a spot of recently tilled dirt with some weeds poking through.

I had to admit, it was sad.

As I stood over the plot, closing my eyes and saying a silent prayer for Tommy, my concentration was broken by the sound of Tommy's grandmother's voice, seeming to pierce my eardrums like an icepick.

As I opened my eyes, there she was, standing about twenty feet away, leaning on an old walking stick, unsteady on her feet. She didn't look so tough now, just like Tommy hadn't looked so tough lying on a slab at the county morgue.

She said, "So, mister tough guy cop, your conscience finally catching up with you?"

I said, "I was just paying my respects is all."

She said, "I find that hard to believe."

I said, "Think what you want, I don't rightly give a damn."

She said, "I can believe that. Maybe you really are a cold hearted bastard with no conscience."

I said, "Whatever you say, ma'am. Are there any other unpleasant things you want to tell me? I have things to do."

She said, "Like what? Shoot somebody? You might as well finish off what family I have left."

I said, "If you are referring to your other grandson, he won't have to worry about it, if he stops harrassing us."

She said, "His name is Danny, and he hasn't hurt anyone."

I said, "Yes, but he intends to, I can see it in his eyes."

She said, "They say that the eyes are the key to the soul, tough guy. Maybe you should look in the mirror next time you feel all high and mighty enough to kill somebody."

I didn't say anything in reply, I just turned and walked toward the cemetery gates. As I reached the gate, I heard her say, "Just remember, tough guy, karma can be a real fickled bitch sometimes."

As I walked through the gates, I thought, glumly, *Yes, I know this all too well.*

#

When I got home, the feeling of emptiness was almost unbearable.

Gone were the days when I came home to my girls running to greet me, and my wife standing in the kitchen, no doubt whipping up something great to eat for dinner, her big smile and bright blue eyes lighting up the room.

Gone were the days when my big, half breed mutt of a dog, Benny, would greet me at the door, licking my face and begging me for doggy treats. He had passed away from old age several months ago, leaving yet another empty void in my heart.

I sat down on the patio, my legs sore from

walking and my stomach empty from hunger. But it wasn't a craving for food, it was the gut wrenching, mind bending craving for the demon alcohol.

I stood up and suddenly felt dizzy, unsteady on my feet, and after righting myself, ventured back into the kitchen to pour myself a a drink – only to realize I had no vodka left.

Another blackout spell, no doubt, making me forget that I needed to make a run to the liquor store.

So, off I went.

#

I drove my old but trustworthy Chevy down to the liquor store, and who did I see upon pulling into the parking lot but Chief Crow, in the flesh.

He'd see me already, so it was too late to leave, so I pulled into the lot, parking right next to his Sedan as he was getting ready to climb in and leave. Upon seeing me, though, he had decided to strike up a conversation about why I was at a liquor store instead of an AA meeting or therapy session.

As I climbed out of the Chevy, he stood there shaking his head and said, ""And just what in the *hell* are you doing at a liquor store, Ben?"

My mind racing, I said, jokingly, "I could ask you the same question."

Crow said, "I'm buying a bottle of wine to have with dinner, if it's any of your concern. Then again, I'm not the one on suspension for a drinking problem."

I lied and said, "I came down here for a pack of cigarettes, sir. That's all."

Crow said, "The 7-11 down the street is closer.

Why not go there?"

I said, "Old habits, I guess. It's no big deal, sir, really."

Crow studied my face for a moment and said, "Well, I guess there's no harm done. But make sure that cigarettes is *all* you buy in there, comprende?"

I said, "Yes, sir. No problem."

Crow climbed into his Sedan and pulled out of the lot, and I waved goodbye to him as he passed by, and, after he was well out of sight, walked inside to buy my cigarettes – and a half gallon of vodka.

Then I drove home, sticking to the side streets and alleys, trying to stay out of sight.

Just like all hopeless, heart broken, desperate drunks tend to do – do their best to avoid their own sad reality.

#

I spent the rest of the day and evening sitting on the patio, sipping my bottle and hoping Veronica would call to check in on me, but I just ended up drunk with no phone calls as to my personal welfare.

I couldn't blame her, though.

What woman in their right mind would want to sit chatting with the man who seemed intent on slowly but surely watching his marriage slip away and embarrass his children?

But I would have done anything to hear her voice and hear my girls tell me they still loved me.

That is, anything but stop drinking.

Each and every time my mind would begin leaning back toward a state of reality, I would grab the bottle and run away like a scared rabbit.

A rabbit with a *habit*.

I knew it was high time to get my shit together and fly right, but I just couldn't shake the monkey off my back.

So I drink, wander around the house, and try to find things to occupy my time – and my mind.

#

I needed to clean my gun.

Glancing around, I noticed that I needed to clean house too, but, currently suffering from a crippling vodka hangover, I opted to sit at the kitchen table and clean my gun instead.

I picked up my gun case and retrieved the tools of the trade; bristle brush, bore rod, and oily rag. I pick up the gun to clean it and my hands are shaking so bad I drop it on the floor, almost landing on my foot.

I know this isn't going to cut it so I open the fresh bottle of vodka sitting on the table and I pour three fingers into an old jelly jar and sip slowly at first, then faster as I realize slow-sipping isn't going to cut it, either.

By the time half of the bottle is gone, I'm ready to clean the gun. Or I thought I was.

Instead, I slipped my gun into my waistband, grabbed my bottle, and retired to the patio for some more reflection.

As I sat in my old lawn chair, staring at the other chair – Veronica's old chair – that terrible, empty feeling took over again...but not for long.

As I sat there almost in a trance like state, sipping

my drink, the sudden sound of a pair of boots adorned with heel caps broke my concentration, and before I could even turn around to see who was approaching my patio after dark, Danny Wallace came into view.

Clad in dirty boots, faded jeans, a flannel shirt and a leather jacket, he was not only the visual poster boy for rednecks, but the personification of death incarnate, his evil little beady eyes staring right through me, as he casually sat down in Veronica's chair, crossed his legs, folded his hands on his lap, and just sat staring at me – right through me – into my very soul.

For some reason I couldn't explain, I just said "Want a drink?"

He said, "You're offering me a drink instead of a bullet? You must be drunk."

I said, "I don't like to drink alone. It's not good for the soul."

He said, "If anybody would know about that, it would be you. Sure, I'll have a drink."

I used an empty plastic cup from the patio table to pour him a drink, and scooted it across the table top, as I kept my mind tuned to the fact I had my .357 in my belt. He picked it up, sipping it, and said, "Not too bad. A little on the cheap side, though. I figured a big hero cop like yourself would buy the good stuff."

I sipped my own drink and said, "I buy what's affordable."

He sipped his drink again, and said, "Been there, done that."

I said, "Just why are you here, anyway, Mister Wallace? I didn't figure us to be too compatible as drinking buddies."

He smiled and said, "To be honest? I'm not sure

why I dropped by. I was just out driving around in the Ford, and found myself in this neck of the woods, thought I'd check in on you, I guess."

I said, sarcastically, "Well, that's mighty friendly of you."

He said, "We ain't friends, and never will be."

I said, "Then why the visit? There must have been something that drew you here."

He sipped his drink and said, "I guess I was just curious as to whether you'd blown your own brains out yet, save me the trouble."

I said, "And just why would I want to blow my own brains out, when I could just blow *your* brains out, and do the world a favor?"

He drained his cup, dropped it on the ground, and said, "Yeah, I see that hand cannon you got in your waistband. The question is, are you man enough to use it, when you're "off duty" that is."

I pulled the .357, cocked the hammer back, pointed it right at his ugly face, and said, "*Try* me."

He just sat there for a few moments, glaring at me hatefully, staring right *through* me, into my soul again. He said, "Thanks for the drink."

Then he stood up, lit a cigarette, and strolled away into the darkness, and out of sight, as I kept my gun trained on him until I was sure he was gone.

Then I drained my glass, refilled it, and just sat there for a while longer, in the moonlight, wondering if I would be better off dead.

#

I woke up around daylight, having pissed myself again.

I staggered inside, made my way to the downstairs bathroom, and voided my guts into the toilet, the dry heaves leaving my throat raw and swollen.

When I was finished, I half walked-crawled to our bedroom – my and Veronica's bedroom – and poured myself into the bed, and didn't wake up until I'd experienced yet another vivid nightmare – this one about Tommy Wallace again, of course.

#

I didn't need Danny Wallace or his grandmother to torture me psychologically, I could handle that all on my own.

In the dream, I was at Tommy's funeral, standing in line to view him before leaving the service. As I approached the casket, Tommy sat bolt upright in the casket, reached out with his gnarled, skeletal hands, grabbed me by the shirt collar, and pulled me close, close enough to smell his foul breath; the odor of the grave, moldy earth and wilted orchids.

He spoke to me, his voice tinged with time and rot, as though he'd been dead for a long time. In a way, I guess he had been, considering his life style.

He said, *Don't worry, Ben Striker. I'll be waiting for you on the other side.*

That's when I woke up screaming.

#

I was beginning to have these nightmares almost every time I was lucky enough to fall asleep.

Or pass out, whichever came first.

At least when I passed out, in a blackout state, I couldn't remember my dreams.

But I was also beginning to realize that if I, myself, or my family was to be safe and secure, Danny Wallace would have to *die*.

That thought was almost more terrifying than my nightmares.

#

The next day, I woke up early, but it wasn't because I was getting any really good sleep, it was because I had *plans* for that day.

Nefarious plans. Wicked, *criminal* plans, that I was hoping would take care of my problem.

My family's problem.

As I sat on the patio, sipping some black coffee, my mind racing with how, exactly, I was going to take care of Danny, my cell phone rang.

It was Crow.

I reluctantly answered the call, and said, "Yes, boss?"

Crow said, "Just wanted you to know, Danny Wallace has been arrested. A patrol officer stopped him near your mother in law's house, in possession of a firearm."

My heart racing, I said, "So, my family is okay?"

Crow said, "Yes, Ben, they're fine."

I breathed a sigh of relief and said, "I think I'll call Veronica today."

Crow said, "I bet she would like that."

I said, "Thanks for everything, boss. I really mean that."

Crow said, "I know you do. Now, make that call." He hung up, and I dialed my mother in law's number. After several rings, it was Veronica that answered.

She said, "Yes, Ben?"

I said, "So, I understand that we got lucky."

She said, "How so? What if his grandma bails him out? By what I understand, she conjures up money like it grows on trees."

I said, "He's a convicted felon, dear. In the possession of a gun."

She said, "And I'm married to a cop, remember? I know how the law works."

I said, "Can we *please* talk about something pleasant or positive for a change?"

She said, "Sure. As soon as that crazy son of a bitch is locked up forever, and you are *sober.*"

Then she hung up.

My heart felt as though it would break in two as I heard that audible *click!* - and the anger and hopelessness behind it.

But she was right about one thing; until a man like Danny Wallace was either locked up forever – or *dead* – it would never really end.

So, it was back to my "plan B" for the time being, whatever that would entail.

Deep down I knew what it would entail, but didn't want to face the cold hard facts of the situation.

Either Danny stayed locked up, or he would have

to die.

I saw no other solution to the problem.

#

Which would mean, of course, I would have to be the one who ended his life.

Just like I'd ended his brother's life.

Would I be able to pull the trigger on his grandmother if need be, too?

I thought so, especially if I was given no other choice.

That afternoon, I was informed that Danny had made bail.

That was all I needed to know; it was time to end this nightmare once and for all.

#

The rest of that day and evening, I sat on the patio, sipping liquid courage and finishing the process of cleaning my gun. I wanted it to be in perfect working order when the time came I put a bullet through Danny's skull.

Now, all I had to do was come up with the most important – and difficult – part of my plan; how to entice Danny into a situation in which I would *have* to shoot him in *self defense.*

Like my wife said, I'm a *cop,* so I knew I could figure out some way to get the job done.

I wanted my *family* back.

I wanted my *life* back.

I wanted Danny Wallace *dead.*

I knew what I had to do.

#

The next day, I sipped black coffee as long as I could, then, in late afternoon, switched to something a bit stronger to build up my courage again.

I needed steady nerves if I was to go through with my plans.

My plan to hunt down Danny Wallace like an animal, and end his miserable life.

Then again, it was hard to compare him to an animal; animals only kill when it is for the purpose of self preservation. A lot of humans, on the other hand, kill because they *enjoy* the act of killing.

I was looking at my own situation as an act of self preservation for me and my family.

I had to come up with *something* to justify taking his life.

But, first things first; the *hunt*.

#

One thing I had to remember was, Danny Wallace caused pain. This was his gift in life. He inflicted pain without remorse or regret.

He *enjoyed* the act.

Therefore, he *needed* to die, to save other innocent people's lives.

Danny had learned at an early age that love was malicious. Love was malice and malice love. He had learned this as a young boy, watching his father beat his younger brother to death.

But, that gave him no right to take other people's lives.

That is where I would step in, and end the seemingly endless cycle of misery and death.

Tonight.

#

I waited until after dark, gased up the old Chevy, made sure I had my .357 tucked away in my waistband, and hit the road.

As a cop, it had always been my knowledge felons tended to associate with other felons, whether it be a bar, a parking lot, just wherever they decided to converge at the time to exchange their tall tales of what a badass they were and how the cops were shit.

One such location was the Third Base tavern, a local hangout that only the bravest of souls dare enter.

The Third Base was a place for only the toughest of the tough, the baddest of the bad, the most felonious of all, and if you didn't fit in, you'd most likely end up on the wrong end of a gun barrel, and your ruined body found later inside a dumpster.

The perfect place for me to hunt for Danny.

As I pulled up out back, in the blood stained, trash littered, gravel parking lot, sure enough, there was Danny's pickup, parked near the back entrance.

I couldn't believe my luck.

I shut off the engine, turned off my lights, and leaned back in the driver's seat, in the pitch black darkness, and waited for Danny.

As I sat there in the dark, sipping from a half pint and chain smoking menthol cigarettes, Danny suddenly burst through the back door, half-staggering down the stairs into the gravel lot, lighting a cigarette and cursing under his breath.

It was perect set-up for me.

I quietly exited the Chevy, walked up behind him as he keyed his truck, tapped him on the shoulder, and when he wheeled around to face me, I gave him a hard right hook to the face.

He yelped and went down hard, on his back, holding his face in his hands, as blood began pouring from his nose and mouth.

Looming over him with my fists balled up, I said, "Come on, tough guy. Get up, and face me like a man."

Wiping blood on hus shirt sleeve, Danny spit blood at my feet, and managed to say, "You sucker punched me, you asshole."

I said, "That's not all I intend to do, tough guy. Now get up and fight me like a man, instead of driving by my mother in law's house, frightening defenseless women."

Danny slowly stood to his feet, righted himself, and said, "I ain't gonna fight you."

I said, "Wrong answer," and punched him again, breaking his orbital socket. He went down hard again, yelping like a wounded animal, and trying to sit up. I kicked him in the ribs this time, the audible sound of the bones breaking echoing off the nearby buildings.

Yet, still no attempt to defend himself on Danny's part; he just laid back, moaning in pain, one hand on his face and the other on his ribs.

I leaned down and said, "Yeah, that's what I thought. Unless you have a knife or a gun or some of your beer buddies to back you up, you aren't anything more than a gutless, spineless, punk."

Danny managed to sit up and say, "You know, your old lady is pretty hot for being in her forties. I guess your daughters took after her, too."

If he was trying to enrage me, it worked.

I leaned down again, reared back with my right fist, and hit him so hard it knocked him out cold, the back of his head hitting the gravel.

It wasn't until that very moment, I'd realized that it was Danny, not me, that had won the fight.

I had just beaten an *unarmed* man to a bloody pulp, and had totally failed in my attempt to coerce him into making me pull my gun.

Then, to make matters worse, I glanced up to see some of the regular bar patrons were filing out of the back door now, glaring at me, their fists balled up in anger.

I pulled the .357, cocked the hammer back, and said, "That'll be far enough, gentlemen. Just back off."

They did so, without resistance, which gave me the chance to back up slowly, to my Chevy, climb into the driver's seat, start the engine, and high tailing it out of there before the cops showed up.

As it turned out, they showed up anyway, at my house, an hour later – led by Chief Crow.

#

I'd been sitting on the patio, sipping what was left of my bottle, when Crow came walking around the back of the house, followed by two uniformed officers.

He walked over to me, stood right in front of me, and said, "So, Ben. I heard you were involved in an altercation at the Third Base bar tonight?"

I just sipped my drink and said, "I wouldn't call it an altercation. It wasn't much of a fight."

Crow said, "Yes, I heard that too."

I said, "Why are you here, sir? I'm busy."

Crow said, "Yeah, busy getting drunk, I see. What were you *thinking*, Ben?! Danny Wallace is the hospital, with a broken nose, a broken orbital socket, two busted ribs, and missing two teeth."

I said, "Then I'd say he got off lucky."

Crow said, "Which is more than I can say for you, Ben. Now, stand up, and assume the position. You know the drill."

I stood up and placed my hands behind my back, as one of the young rookie cops placed the cuffs on me. When he was done, Crow said, "Ben Striker, you are being placed under arrest for aggravated assault."

I just took a deep breath, exhaled, and said, "Let's just get this over with so I can bail out in time for bed."

#

Just my luck, the jail was *full*.

The Monroe County jail was no Holiday Inn, either.

Your average drunk tank is just that; a 12 by 15 foot concrete and steel tank, like you'd see at a zoo.

But you won't see any animals in a drunk tank, animals are too intelligent to spend any time in such a dump.

The smells and sounds are the worst part of it all.

Your average drunk tank smells like farts and puke and shit and piss and dirty feet, and the only sounds you normally hear are yelling and snoring and farting and puking.

The only tine a drunk tank even comes close to being tolerable is at night, when the rest of the drunks have finally passed out, and you can finally find a spot to curl up and take a nap yourself – that is, if there are any empty spots left open.

The day I was there, I could find absolutely no empty spots – except a small, cramped spot right next to the toilet stall.

Not your ideal spot for napping, but I had no choice that day.

So, I curled up like a cozy kitten between the stall wall and the toilet, and hoped and prayed for the best.

In my current – and drunken – frame of mind, I hadn't anticipated the fact that one or more of my fellow jailbirds might need to use the toilet.

As it turned out, between the hours of midnight and four am, there were at least five guys that need to relieve themselves, and three of them needed to void their bowels.

Luckily, though, that's about the time one of the jail guards came back there and informed me it as time for me to bail out.

#

At the release desk, as I signed the obligatory paperwork and gathered my personal belongings – minus any bottles, of course – Crow came walking down the hallway, and once I'd signed the release form, he said, "I did you a favor tonight, Ben. So do *NOT* let me down."

I said, "A favor? How do you see it that way?"

Crow said, "Well, for one thing, I had you placed in the drunk tank, instead of in the general population cells. There were most likely men in there you have arrested in the past."

After mulling it over, I said, "Yeah, that was probably a good thing."

Crow said, "Secondly, I marked your name off of the court docket. You won't have to appear in court, or have your name in the local newspaper."

I said, "Why are you doing this for me, boss? I don't really deserve it."

Crow said, "I'm not doing it for *you*, I'm doing it for your *family*. They don't deserve this, either."

He was right about that. I said, "So, where do we go from here?"

Crow said, "*We* don't go anywhere. *You* go home, get some rest – some *sober* rest – and be at my office day after tomorrow, at ten am sharp."

I said, "Why? So you fire me and get it over with?"

Crow said, "If I had any common sense, I would fire you right here and now. But I guess I have a soft spot for good cops with a monkey on their back."

I said, "Thank you, boss."

Crow said, "Don't thank me, thank your wife. And your kids. If it wasn't for them being in the picture, I would have fired your ass."

I said, "Yes, sir. Sorry."

Crow said, "Don't apologize to me, save your lame excuses for your wife. Now, go on home, sober up, and act like a man. Like the cop you *used* to be."

Then he walked away.

I stood there for a few seconds, my eyes filling up

with tears, then walked away as well.

#

Crow had my old Chevy waiting for me in the impound lot, unlocked and ready to go.

Yet another favor I hadn't deserved.

But, not wanting to spend any unnecessary time looking a gift horse in the mouth, I hopped in, started the engine, and headed toward home, post haste.

#

When I got home, it was almost five am.

Well past my usual bedtime, but after spending a few hours in the drunk tank, I was sure it wouldn't take me long to go to sleep.

I was wrong.

By six am, I was still awake, sitting at the kitchen table – but sipping coffee this time.

Black coffee.

No additives.

It was rough, but I hung in there, for better or worse.

As it turned out, it was for the worse.

But only temporarily.

#

By that afternoon, I was having withdrawl symptoms, but by early evening, I was slowly but surely getting back on an even keel, and was able to choke down some food and liquids – other than alcohol, that is.

I was still feeling rough, but I figured that just came with the territory, so I stuck with it, got my shit wired tight and my brain focusing on *positive* things, like staying sober, and getting my family back.

I wasn't worried about being a cop any more; I was sure I could still support my family without having to risk my life every day for lousy pay.

But, first things first.

The ability to make *sober* decisions.

#

I hadn't slept well that night either, but knew I had to make that appointment with Crow.

After a long hot shower and about a gazillion cups of black coffee, I was ready.

I hoped so, anyway.

As I stopped at his office door and knocked, I could feel my stomach begin to lurch again like it had the night before, and had to fight with all of my being not to vomit as a deep, gruff voice coming from inside the office said, "Come in."

Taking a deep breath, I walked in to see Crow sitting at his desk drinking coffee. He said, "You don't look so good. Need some coffee?"

Feeling my guts begin to lurch again, I did my best to not throw up, and said, "No thanks. I've had enough coffee over the last thirty six hours to choke a horse."

Crow cracked a grin and said, "I know a bad hangover when I see one. It's in the eyes, the pallor of your skin, the shaky hands. You're getting ready to take the walk of shame, and you're so nervous that you feel like you could throw up. Am I correct in my assumption?"

I said, glumly, "Yes, sir. But, the walk of shame?"

Crow said, "Yes, the walk of shame. The walk you're getting ready to take when you leave my office."

Swallowing a lump in my throat, I said, "Sir?"

Crow said, "Don't worry, you're not fired – although you should be. But, God knows, if I had always fired a good cop for having a monkey on their back, half of my department would be flipping burgers at Wendy's."

I said, "I know I've asked this question before, sir, but where do we go from here?"

He sipped his coffee, stood up, and said, "It's where *you* go from here, officer Striker. First of all, I'm placing you on another one month suspension, without pay for the first two weeks. You will also see the department shrink during this time period, as well as attending AA meetings indefinitely. At the end of your suspension, if I feel as though you still have a monkey on your back, you will take the walk of shame for the *last* time. Are we clear on this matter?"

Breathing a sigh of relief, I said, "Yes, sir. Crystal clear, sir."

Crow sat back down and said, "Besides, just between you and me? I have been in your shoes too, early in my career. Somebody gave me a second chance, too. But that's our little secret, right?"

Cracking a grin, I said, "Just between you and me, sir, yes."

Crow said, "Fine, then. Now, go get your shit together, officer Striker."

It was around noon when I got back home, and as soon as I walked through the door, the land line portable was ringing.

I got to it just in time, to hear Veronica's voice on the other end of the line. I felt my heart skip a beat as she said, "Hello, Ben."

I said, "It's good to hear your voice."

She said, "Ditto."

I said, "How are you? And the girls?"

She said, "We're fine, Ben. The girls keep asking me when we're going home, though. I told them it was up to you."

I said, "Meaning, how long I can stay sober."

She said, "What do you expect, Ben?"

I said, sadly, "I know it's my fault, Veronica. But you don't have to rub salt in an open wound."

She said, "Fair enough. So, are you at least *attempting* to stay sober?"

I said, "Almost three days now. That's not bad, considering."

She said, "Yes, that's good. I'm proud of you, Ben. I really am."

I said, "Well, I'm doing it for you and the girls."

She said, "Ben, you have to want to do it for *yourself*, first."

I said, "This is true."

She said, "Thank you. Well, I better get off of here and get motivated. I'm taking the girls to the mall today."

I said, "Let me guess; to the TJ Maxx and then for ice cream?"

She said, "Why of course."

I said, "Veronica?"

She said, "Yes, Ben?"

I said, "I love you."

She said, "Ditto," and hung up.

I hung up too, wishing I was anywhere but in that cold lonely house by myself.

But I wasn't alone for long.

#

I had poured a cup of black coffee and grabbed a pack of smokes before heading out to the patio, to find no other than grandma Wallace sitting out there, in Veronica's chair.

Before I could even utter a word in protest, she spoke up and said, "So, tough guy cop. Been beating the hell out of any unarmed men lately?"

I said, "I had no way of knowing he was unarmed, and he was acting in a threatening manner."

She said, "He said you sucker punched him."

I said, "That's bullshit."

She said, "I doubt that. You see, my grandsons have had their faults, I'll grant you that. But one of their faults hasn't included being a liar."

I said, "No, their most valuable character trait has been being a couple of homicidal maniacs."

She said, "You're just a crooked cop who drinks too much and hurts innocent folks because you enjoy it. So, what does that make you?"

I stepped closer and said, "I didn't have a drinking problem until I met Tommy. And you know what? I don't feel so guilty any more. As a matter of fact, now that I look back on that day, I *am* really glad that I shot him. The world is a better place without him."

His grandma stood up, glaring at me hatefully, and said, "Best watch your nasty mouth, boy. Danny will be healed up soon enough."

I said, "And I can't wait to see him again. As a matter of fact, tell him I said to pack his lunch next time, because he's going to need it, it's going to be an all day beat down."

She smiled, lit a cigarette, and said, "I'll let him know."

I said, "I can't wait."

She turned to leave, and as she reached the patio gate, she turned around and said, "Oh, and mister Striker?"

I said, "Yes, ma'am?"

She said, "You best pack your lunch, too."

#

I called Crow immediately to inform him of her visit.

He answered on the fourth ring, and said, "This better be good. I was about to eat my lunch late as it is."

I said, "Grandma Wallace paid me a visit."

Crow said, "Stubborn old bat, isn't she?"

I said, "You have absolutely no idea."

Crow said, "Sorry, Ben. So, has she made any death threats? Well, you get the idea."

I said, "Unfortunately, no, she hasn't. All she said by the way of an indirect threat was that Danny was already healing up, and he wasn't very happy about the situation."

Crow said, "Well, like grandmother, like

grandson. Did you know that Tommy shot her own son, his father?”

I said, “Yes, I knew all about it. Yet, she still defends anything her grandsons take part in. I think the whole family tree is insane.”

Crow said, “Not necessarily. Some folks are just born ornery and mean.”

I said, “Well, regardless of whatever category they fall into, I'm still a little paranoid.”

Crow said, “Don't be. That's what they want, to be able to catch you off guard.”

I said, “Well, I wish them luck, now that I'm sober.”

Crow said, “Yeah, well, just *stay* that way, and you should be fine.”

I said, “Yes sir, boss.”

Crow said, “It's lunch time, Striker. Go eat.”

He hung up.

I hung up too, and suddenly realized how hungry I really was.

#

I ended up eating breakfast for lunch; two eggs, two slices of bacon, and toast with strawberry jam.

And black coffee, of course.

By then, I was so sick of black coffee that just the thought of it made me nauseous.

So I looked in the icebox for my other choices; outdated orange juice, or sour milk.

I stuck with the coffee.

#

Knowing it was high time for a shopping trip, I freshened up and took a drive down to the corner market, Cash N Dash, for a few items to tide me over.

Since I was still alone at the house for now, I had picked out the obligatory bachelor cuisine; bread, milk, sandwich meat, cereal, several microwave dinners, and some takeout chicken.

As I approached the register, the short, petite, pretty little blond {I never knew her real name, so I just called her Blondie} was standing there, wearing a big smile as usual, friendly and sociable, an asset to her place of employment.

I said, "Well, hello, sugar pop," I said, placing my items on the counter. "You're not working in the kitchen today?"

She said, "I'm doing double duty today."

I said, "You can handle it, I have faith in you."

She just smiled and said, "Aw...thank you."

As she bagged up my items, I swiped my credit card through the little thingie and placed it back in my wallet, and she said, "Oh, I almost forgot. Some guy was in here asking about you yesterday."

I said, "Some guy? What did he look like?"

She said, "I really didn't pay much attention, except he had a bandage on his head and face, like he'd been in an accident."

Danny, I thought, feeling my guts tighten up. I said, "Did he leave his name?"

She said, "Nope, sorry, Ben."

I said, "What did he say, exactly?"

She said, "Not much, just asked if I knew who you were, and if I'd seen you lately. I didn't know what to say, so I didn't say *anything*."

I said, "Good girl."

She said, "Should I be worried? He looked at me awful funny. It gave me the creeps."

As I grabbed my bags from the counter, I said, "You don't have anything to worry about. I'll let the local police know just in case."

As I walked outside, I couldn't help but feel as though the pretty little blonde was going to be Danny's next target, having given up on the idea of stalking my family for now.

Which, of course, meant that he was still keeping tabs on me, where I went, who I talked to, etc.

I called Crow as soon as I got home.

#

Needless to say, he was less than thrilled with the situation.

After I told him about my trip to Cash N Dash, he said, "Ben, I understand your concern for that young lady, really I do. But you can't do anything for her, that is, *outside* of the law. I'll place extra patrols there when she's working, okay? But *you* need to back *off*."

I said, "I hadn't intended to get involved. I was just relaying to you that she might be in danger." *A lie.*

Crow said, "That's a good thing, because I don't think I could defend your actions in a court of law if you *shot* someone while you're *suspended* from duty."

I said, "I'm not stupid, boss."

Crow said, "No, you're not. So don't *act* like you are, and allow this situation to get to you."

I said, "So, an extra patrol on the days she

works?"

Crow said, "Yes. I'll make a call to her employer today, and let them know."

I said, "Thanks, boss."

Crow said, "Just remember what I said."

He hung up.

After I hung up, I still couldn't help but feel as though I was going to be thrust head first into another situation like I'd been in the day Tommy Wallace died.

I was hoping and praying I was wrong.

#

I had been in the kitchen, putting away the rest of my grocery items and sipping black coffee again, when I heard a knock at my door.

When I opened the door, it was Crow standing there, holding my badge and service weapon.

He said, "Can I talk to you for a few minutes?"

My eyes still fixed on my badge and gun, I said, "Of course, come on in."

Crow walked into the kitchen, took a seat at the table, and placed the badge and gun on the table top. He lit a cigarette and said, "I want to reinstate you as a police officer."

I thought I was dreaming all of it. I said, "Why the change of heart?"

Crow said, "I've been thinking, why waste a good cop when there are so many assholes running around loose out there?"

I said, "You mean, assholes like Danny Wallace?"

Crow just grinned and said, "I didn't say that, you did."

I said, "So, I suppose there are certain conditions that come with my reinstatement?"

Crow said, "None except for the obvious; stay sober and clean, attend your AA meetings."

I said, "Fair enough."

Crow said, "Alright, then." He scooted the badge and gun across the table to me. I picked them up, and they felt good in my hands.

I felt like I had been...*reborn.*

I said, "Thanks, boss."

Crow said, "Just don't let me down."

He stood up and walked toward the front door and I followed. As he walked out, he turned back to me and said, "Oh, and by the way, I hear Danny Wallace has been hanging around the local Cash N Dash. You might want to let him know that he's not welcome there."

Then he walked away without another word.

There weren't really any words that needed to be spoken.

#

Later that evening, I set about taking part in my first stakeout of the Cash N Dash.

There was a perfect hiding spot right across the street, in the parking lot used for the local hospital. Plenty of bushes and tall shrubbery, and a few cars I could park behind as I watched the place.

The first night, I didn't see much other than the usual that time of night; last minute customers coming in for cigarettes or microwave snacks or leftover chicken from the kitchen.

No sign of Danny, though.

Then again, he was a sly, sneaky little shit, so he could have been hiding somewhere close by, just like me, waiting for the right moment to strike.

To kidnap the pretty blonde? To do so just to force my hand and show myself?

The very thought of it made my guts tighten up in knots, and my blood boil.

So I sat, and waited.

A few minutes later, a car pulled up, a small Sedan, and a few seconds later here came Blondie, all smiles and waving at the driver of the car, an older lady with short blonde hair, possibly her mother.

Blondie hopped into the front passenger's seat and they pulled out of the lot, with nobody tailing them.

First night; so far, so good.

#

The next day, before heading back to the stakeout, I called Crow to fill him in on my current agenda.

After filling him in, I had taken a quick shower, dressed in my street clothes {my uniforms were currently sitting at the local dry cleaners} grabbed a thermos full of coffee and a pack of cigarettes, and headed back to the Cash N Dash.

I got there around ten thirty am, when the early lunch crowd was packing in there for the chicken dinners, and parked in the same spot I'd been in the night before.

As I sat there smoking a cigarette and sipping lukewarm coffee, I could see Blondie, through the front window, running around as busy as a bee, chatting and smiling and, in general, just being her charming self.

The thought of Danny kidnapping her and doing unspeakable things to her crossed my mind again, and I did my best to block the thought from my mind.

I had to keep my mind clear, my shit wired tight, as Crow would say.

It was the *only* way.

#

As the lunch time crowd thinned out, my cell phone rang, and it was Veronica.

I said, "Yes, dear? To what do I owe this special call?"

She said, "Okay, mister smartass."

I said, jokingly, "So, how was the shopping trip with the girls? Will we still be able to afford Christmas this year?"

She said, "You're a real smartass today, aren't you?"

I said, "I was just joking. So, how did it go?"

She said, "The same as usual. The girls arguing over what outfit was the coolest or what boy band was the cutest at the record store. I told them that both outfits were equally cool, and that boy bands were much too nineties for them."

I said, "Sorry I missed that."

She said, "Me too."

I said, "So, is there anything particular you want to talk about?"

She said, "Just wanted to hear your voice, that's all."

I said, "Well, that's a good thing, right?"

She said, "That depends."

I said, "If you are referring to me still being on the wagon, I haven't fallen off yet."

She said, "Well, that's a good thing."

I said, "Why don't you come by sometime soon, with the girls, and we'll order a pizza?"

She said, "It's a date."

I said, "Good. Well, I better go for now, I'm on the job."

She said, "Yes, I heard."

I said, "Crow has a big mouth."

She said, "Yes, but at least it was *good* news this time."

I said, "This is true."

She said, "Love you babe."

I said, "Ditto."

She giggled and hung up. I did the same, and turned my attention back to the Cash N Dash.

#

Around three pm, with the lunch time crowd long gone, the place was still busy, but not so much I couldn't keep a watchful eye on Blondie through the windows.

After taking another peek with my department issued binoculars, I placed them on the seat beside me, lit another smoke, and leaned back to rest my eyes a bit.

My old Chevy has been designed to look good, but the seats had apparently not been designed to feel good. My back was killing me, and I needed a break.

I craned my head to take a look in front of me, behind me, and left to right, and not seeing Danny anywhere in sight, I decided to take a quick stroll to the Cash N Dash for some fresh coffee and a big juicy donut.

As I walked to the register, I could see Blondie was working the counter at the time, which was a good thing, because I had a question for her.

As she rung up the sale, I said, "So, have you seen Mr creepy again?

She said, "Nope, and I don't care if I do, either."

I leaned in and whispered, "I don't blame you. But don't worry, I am right across the street, if I'm needed."

She glanced across the street to see my car, smiled, and said, "Thanks."

I said, "No problem. Now, how about my police officer discount on the donut?"

#

I didn't get a donut discount, but she did offer me a free refill on the coffee if I needed one.

As I sat there again, in the old Chevy, eyeballing the Cash N Dash parking lot, I got bored listening to the radio, turned it off, and breathed a sigh of relief.

Stakeouts were like that; the things you thought you were lucky to have around to occupy your time sometimes became mundane, very boring after so many hours went by.

By the time Blondie had left work, in the safe, loving arms of the lady in the Sedan, it was just in time; I was nodding off in the driver's seat.

#

That night, I slept like a baby; no nightmares, no late night phone calls, no tossing and turning.

The demon alcohol had finally lost the battle for my soul.

I was *me* again.

\#

The next morning, I parked in my usual spot, and was sipping coffee and having a smoke when I glanced up to see none other than Danny Wallace, his face still swollen a bit and walking with a limp, walking across the back lot of the Cash N Dash.

I was out of the Chevy and sprinting across the street like a pro athlete in a heartbeat.

I reached the back lot just as he was getting ready to enter the back door. I said, loudly, "No, Danny. Just back away from the door right now."

He turned around slowly, looking me directly in the eyes, and said, "Well, if it ain't the neighborhood hero."

I said, "I'm not going to keep repeating myself, Danny. I said, back away from the door."

He reluctantly backed away, as other customers filed by, flashing him an apprehensive look. He said, "So, I see you got your badge back."

I said, "And my gun too." I reached behind me, into my waistband, and pulled out my service weapon, a nine millimeter Glock.

Danny said, "What? No hand cannon?"

I said, "Oh believe me, my Glock will do just

fine."

Danny said, "Ain't got no doubt about that, after what you did to Tommy."

I lowered the weapon, took a deep breath, and said, "No more of your bullshit, Danny. As of right now, you've been trespassed from this building, and, you are to have no contact at all, with the young lady that works the front counter. Do you understand?"

Danny said, "Or what? You gonna shoot me?"

I stepped closer, and aimed the Glock right at his face, and said, "Don't even try me, Danny. I'll put a bullet through your head, and go back home and sleep like a baby."

Danny said, "I bet you would at that."

I said, "Then why are you still standing here?"

Danny slowly backed away, from the building and myself, keeping his eye trained on my gun. When he reached the end of the lot, he stopped and said, "Like I said before, this ain't over. You can count on that."

I said, "Oh, I am counting on it. I can't wait to put a bullet right through your crazy, diseased brain."

With that, Danny snickered, flipped me the middle finger, and walked away.

I placed my gun back in my waistband, took another deep breath, exhaled, and walked back to my car and climbed into the driver's seat.

I was shaking like a leaf in a high wind, my whole body feeling cold and clammy.

It was then I realized just how close I *really* came to killing another human being – and feeling no guilt about it whatsoever.

#

After hanging around for a few more hours, and being sure that Blondie was picked up safely, I'd gone home to a TV dinner, a glass of tea, and a movie on Netflix.

I was missing Veronica and my girls so bad.

After tossing part of my TV dinner into the trash, I picked up my cell phone from the coffee table and called my mother in law's place. Her mother answered the phone. She said, "She's not here, Ben."

I said, "Do you know when she'll be back?"

She said, "No, I don't. She and the girls left a few hours ago."

I thought, *No doubt on another shopping trip to pacify the girls*. I said, "Would you give her a message for me?"

She said, "I guess so."

I said, "Tell her I called, and was wanting to know what night she wanted to order a pizza for the girls."

She said, "Okay."

I said, "Well, you have a good evening."

She said, "You too."

She hung up, and I did the same, but feeling empty inside as always.

Without my Veronica.

We both knew that we would be together forever, and most people described our relationship as a fairy tale come true. Like you'd read in a book or watch in a movie.

Except for her mother.

She had always worried about my choice of profession, was always afraid I would get killed in the line of duty, and leave her only daughter a widow.

The same thought had crossed my mind, too, but I

had already committed to it. Back then, Veronica had been proud of me for my choice of profession, had even respected me for it – that is, until I met up with Tommy Ray Wallace.

That's when my – *our* whole life – seemed to fall apart before our eyes.

God, how I needed Veronica that night.

I was hoping she still needed me, too.

#

I stayed up fairly late just in case she called back, and, after receiving no call back by around midnight, I'd gone to bed, knowing I had another long day tomorrow.

More sitting and staring at the Cash N Dash through a pair of binoculars, watching out for Blondie, making sure she was okay, and making sure Danny kept his distance.

I was beginning to *hate* him.

Despise and loathe him.

He was like a thorn buried deep in my side, an itch I couldn't scratch.

But most of all, I was sure he was planning to harm someone close to me in the future, and I couldn't bear that thought.

I would have given my *own* life to prevent that, if need be.

So, the next morning, I climbed into the old Chevy once again and drove back to the stakeout.

To my destiny?

Only time would tell.

#

I hadn't been sitting there long when Crow called me to check in on my progress.

He said, "So, Ben. How's the so called stakeout going?"

I said, "So far so good. I had a little visit from Danny yesterday, in the parking lot, but I convinced him it would be in his best interest to leave the premises."

Crow said, "*How* did you convince him? You know we want a *righteous* bust on this one. No more kicking ass and asking questions later."

That word, *righteous*. It almost got stuck in my throat now, like a bad taste in my mouth, choking me. I said, "Don't worry, boss. He left here in one piece, his cocky attitude included."

Crow said, "Good, that's what we want. Let him hang himself this time."

I said, "I'd like to hang him by his testicles."

Crow said, "Down, boy. Behave yourself."

I said, "I'm doing my best."

Crow said, "Good, and keep it that way."

I said, "Yes, sir."

Crow said, "Have a good day, Ben."

I said, "Same to you," and hung up.

#

About an hour later, as I sat sipping coffee and taking periodic peeks at the back lot with my binoculars, it happened.

My destiny.

As I was scanning the back of the building, here came Blondie, carrying out two trash bags to toss in the dumpster. She was light on her feet and sort of hopping and skipping over to the dumpster, without a care in the world. *The naive happiness of youth before it is ripped away.*

And, coming up behind her, carrying a large hunting knife in his left hand, was Danny Wallace.

I was almost frozen stiff in fear and terror at first, but it didn't take long for me to start moving.

I was out of the Chevy and pulling my service weapon and was within twenty feet of them both when I realized I'd never make it in time. I stopped, raised the Glock in the air above my head, and fired a warning shot.

Blondie, startled by the sound, wheeled around and looked me right in the eyes, then she immediately raised her arms up over her head, and ducked down behind the dumpster.

Danny stood there staring at me, *smiling* at me, and raising his left hand in the air, brandishing the knife for all to see. Other customers were filing in and out by then, tapping at their cell phones, no doubt calling 911.

But it was too late for that.

I lowered the Glock, and aimed it right at his head, and said, "Stupid, just like your brother, bringing a knife to a gunfight."

He grinned, spit on the ground, and said, "Hell, a knife is all I need to have fun with sugar pants over there."

Blondie suddenly burst out from behind the dumpster, ran over and ducked down behind me, and said, "I'd rather kiss a toilet seat."

Still grinning, Danny said, "That could be arranged. I like it sorta kinky."

Blondie said, "Screw you, freak."

I said, "Enough of this bullshit, Danny. Drop the knife, or I'll shoot you."

Danny stepped closer, his eyes trained on my own. When I looked into his eyes, I saw nothing there; deep, dark, and empty. No heart or soul. No remorse or empathy. Just an endless, black chasm of emptiness – and evil.

He said, "Yeah, just like you did to my brother, you son of a bitch."

Then he lunged at me, the knife blade shining in the sunlight, almost blinding me.

I pulled the trigger.

Danny went down howling like a wounded animal, yelping and holding his right leg. The bullet had struck him in the right upper thigh, a painful wound, but not a fatal one.

That's when I heard the sirens coming in the distance, Crow no doubt in the lead.

I placed my gun back into my waistband, sat down next to Blondie, and lit a cigarette. She lit one too, and said, "Thanks, Ben."

I waved her off and said, "No problem, sugar pop. I wouldn't have had it any other way."

She said, "Well, you're *my* hero."

I said, jokingly, "Fair enough. But, I expect more free coffee refills from now on."

She smiled and said, "Cool, but I'll toss in a free donut, too."

I said, "Deal."

Then we just sat there and watched as the flashing lights and sirens drowned out Danny's wailing, the sound of it slowly fading away already like a distant memory.

#

As Danny was loaded into the back of an ambulance, and a uniformed officer stood nearby taking a statement from Blondie, I stood chatting with Crow.

Glancing around at all of the mayhem finally coming to and end, Crow said to me, "So, it's over now, I gather?"

I said, "Yes, unless you have another stakeout lined up for me, which I hope isn't on your agenda."

Crow grinned and said, "None I can think of."

I said, "Thank God."

Crow said, "May I ask you a question, and recieve a truthful answer?"

I said, "I'm listening."

Crow said, "Why the leg shot?"

I said, "I wasn't aiming for his leg."

Crow said, "Hmm...maybe a case of divine intervention, then?"

I said, "It could be, I guess. Someone watching over me."

Crow said, "Either that, or fate."

I said, "Or destiny."

Crow said, "Either way, Danny will be old and grey when he gets out of prison, that is, if he lives that long."

I said, "That sounds just peachy with me."

Crow said, "Don't worry about his grandmother, either. I'll handle her."

I said, "The thought hadn't even crossed my mind, but thanks for the sentiment."

Crow said, "You're welcome. Well, I guess I better get motivated, it looks like it's going to be a long day. I hate all this paperwork."

I said, "Me, too."

As Crow walked away into the crowd, he said to me, "Remember to drop by the office in the morning, Ben. For your formal statement, I mean. You know, just department procedure."

I said, "I'll be there bright and early."

As Crow walked away, I sat down on the curb again, lit a smoke, and just sat there as I watched my destiny had come full circle now.

Divine intervention, indeed.

#

I hadn't been at home more than a few minutes when my cell phone rang.

It was Veronica.

It was so good to hear her voice as she said, "I see you were playing hero again this morning."

I said, "Good news travels fast, apparently, in the age of social media."

She said, "*Is* it good news, Ben? Is it *really* all over now?"

I said, "Yes, it is, and, you and the girls still owe me a date for takeout pizza."

She said, "Tomorrow night around seven?"

Feeling my heart beating a little faster, I said, "That would be just peachy."

She said, "See you then."

She hung up, I did the same, and then I sat down at the table to go over my statement for Crow.

I needn't have worried about rehearsing anything for Crow, by then, I knew the whole story by heart.

When I knocked on his office door, I heard his voice, loud and clear, but this time, more subdued, mild in tone. He said, "Come in, Ben."

I opened the door to see Crow sitting behind his desk with a personnel file on his desk top, with my name on it. I said, jokingly, "Well, that could be good, or bad."

Crow said, "What's that?"

I said, "My file on your desk."

Crow said, "It's good, depending on your answer to my next question."

I said, "Which is?"

Crow said, "Have you ever given any thought to working on our detective division?"

I had to admit, the thought had crossed my mind; longer hours, but better pay, and benefits. I said, "The thought has crossed my mind, yes. I've been beating the concrete for a long time."

Crow said, "I know. That's why I think a change of scenery would be good for you, and your family."

I said, "Homicide division, I gather?"

Crow said, "Yes. I think you would be a great addition to the homicide division."

I said, "I hope so, really I do."

Crow said, "Then you'll aceept my offer?"

I said, "Yes, sir. I'd be proud to join your team, sir."

Crow said, "Splendid. And why don't we ditch the

formal monikers in the future, and address each other by our given names?"

I said, "Yes, sir. I mean, Harlan."

Crow said, "Thank you, Ben. Now, go on home and take it easy for the rest of the day."

I said, "I have a date with the wife and girls tomorrow night. May I report in the day after?"

Crow smiled and said, "Yes, of course."

I said, "Thank you."

As I turned to walk away, Crow said, "Ben?"

I said, "Yes?"

Crow said, "It's good to have the old you back again."

I said, "Yes, it is."

#

It was good to have the *old* me back.

As I sat at the kitchen table that night, eating a microwave sandwich and sipping sun tea, I sat staring at the other three empty chairs, knowing soon that my family would soon be sitting there again, just like it used to be before Tommy Wallace entered my life.

I no longer felt guilty, either.

It was a righteous shooting, in the line of duty, and it saved an innocent bystander's life.

Amen.

#

After my sandwich, I walked out on the patio to enjoy some star gazing, unwind before bed time.

As I walked outside, to my utter horror and disbelief, I saw granny Wallace sitting in my wife's lawn chair, smoking a dog turd cigar and sipping a half pint of some sort of cheap liquor.

Upon seeing me, she said, "Well, if it ain't the big hero, who shot the last grandson I had."

Fumbling around with my waistband, I realized I hadn't bothered packing my .357, and felt helpless as I said, "At least he's alive."

She snickered and said, "Yeah, for what it's worth. He'll be lucky to ever see the light of day again, because of you."

I said, "*He* is the one who made that choice, when he wouldn't drop that knife. This happened because of his *own* choices, just like Tommy."

She said, "That's a damn lie, and you know it."

I said, "Speaking of which, maybe you need to stop lying to *yourself.*"

She sat up then, fishing around inside of her little handbag, and pulled out a compact, .22 caliber revolver. She pointed it at me, and said, "You ever see what one of these tiny little twenty two bullets will do to a person's brain? Bounces around inside your skull like a basketball, it does. Of course, you probably know that already."

Standing there frozen in fear, I said, "Yes, I know. I have seen too many people die over the years not to know what it's capable of. Too many *wasted* lives, just like your grandson's life."

She cocked the hammer back on the gun, and said, "You love your wife, Mister hero? Love your girls?"

I said, "Yes, I do. With all my heart and soul."

With tears streaming from her old, tired eyes, she said, "Then I hope you never have to lose them. It makes you feel so...hopeless."

Then she placed the barrel of the .22 against her right temple, and pulled the trigger.

#

One of my neighbors told me later that they could have heard me screaming a block away.

But it was *over* now.

Really over.

The last of the tainted bloodline.

I had realized that day that none of these lost souls I saw on the street every day were *born* that way. Some of them were just unlucky enough – maybe doomed by fate itself – to have been caught up in a situation they had no control over, and their eventual and untimely demise had already been set in motion long *before* they were born.

I had said a silent prayer for the grandmother before I called 911.

#

Needless to say, our date night – and the first day of my new job – had been put on hold, but only briefly.

By the following week, I had started my new detective position, and we had our date night the same day, to celebrate both of the special occasions at the same time.

To my utter surprise – and delight – Veronica had handled the situation like a real trooper, and my girls had too.

My mother in law, Verna, had even called that night and had sent me well wishes on my new job position, which, to me, was a small miracle in itself.

Divine intervention, perhaps?

Only time would tell, with Verna.

#

By that evening, a Friday night with unseasonably pleasant temperatures and a beautiful sunset, I had wanted to conduct our pizza party on the patio, but Veronica had suggested that considering what had taken place there recently, the kitchen table might be more appropriate.

After thinking it over, I'd realized she was right.

No more memories of the PAST.

At least no *bad* ones.

While the girls ate pizza and bread sticks and watched a DVD in the living room, Veronica and I sat in the kitchen doing the same thing, minus the DVD of course.

We had other things to do.

Things it seemed like we hadn't done together in years, but had only been a few weeks.

Like feeling *human* again.

As she sat across from me, nibbling pizza and sipping her iced tea, I said, "Penny for your thoughts, my dear?"

She said, "I was just thinking about us."

I said, jokingly, "Is that good or bad?"

She said, "That depends."

I said, "Uh oh."

She said, "Don't worry, it's something good for a change."

I said, "Such as?"

She said, "Such as, sending the girls over to Lisa's house tonight, so we can be alone."

I said, "Are you actually trying to get frisky with me?"

She said, "And if I am?"

I said, "I think I'm ready for dessert now."

#

Later that evening, as I sat on the patio, in the dark, having a smoke and staring up at the stars, my mind suddenly drifted back to the night I shot Tommy Wallace.

Don't ask me why; I don't have an answer.

No plausible, *normal* answer, that is.

But there it was, in my mind again – as though it had never left.

So, I light another cigarette and sip my tea, as my mind tells me, *It was a righteous kill.*

Will my heart and mind ever stop pulling me in so many different directions? Maybe, maybe not.

I close my eyes and make a wish on the stars in the night sky.

As if my wife can read my mind, she is there now, and she reaches over and grasps my hand gently in her own, gives it a little squeeze, winks at me, and whispers *I love you.*

I say, *I love you, too.*

At that moment, I realize that's all I will ever really need.

David Boyer is a Christian, a multi-genre writer, a true crime buff, and the author of several coming of age novellas, numerous horror and scifi stories, as well as the author of numerous essays including the subjects of government corruption, Christianity, bullying, and cyber-stalking.

He lives in Vincennes, Indiana, with his cat, Holly Jean, who now serves as his copy editor by jumping on the computer keyboard when he's not looking.

Books: {Non-fiction}
True crime:
Small Town Murder: True Crime Stories From Knox County, Indiana
Murder In the Hoosier Heartland: Infamous Indiana Murderers & Fledgling Serial Killers
Murder & Mayhem In the Hoosier Heartland: Mysterious Disappearances & Bizarre Murders In Indiana
The Blitz: A Rape Victim's Story
Vanished In Vincennes: the Mysterious Disappearance and Death Of Dolores Oliver
47 Years of Hell: The Dolores Oliver Murder: Still Unsolved
Small Town Murder In Knox County, Indiana: Hate Crimes, Witch Hunts, and A Definitive List of Indiana Serial Killers
The Guy In The Blue Shirt

Non-fiction: {paranormal, bio & memoir}
Haunted Heartland: Haunted Hoosiers Tell Their Ghost Stories
Strange Happenings In the Hoosier Heartland
I Remember When, In Vincennes…Volume 1
Growing Up In Vincennes – Volumes 2 – 5
The Time of Our Lives: Growing Up Cool In Vincennes, Indiana

Essays:
Bullying: the Road to Recovery and Forgiveness
Privacy In the Age of the Internet: How Sexting and Sharing Private Photos Can lead To Cyber-Stalking
Once An Alcoholic, Always An Alcoholic? The Cold Hard Truth About Our Addictions
Travesties of Jutice: Flaws In Our Legal System That Imprison the Innocent
Will the REAL Christian Please Stand Up?
Racism in the 21ˢᵗ Century: ALL Lives Matter
Conflicted Souls: How the Man In Black Saved My Life
Crossing the Rainbow Bridge: Saying Goodbye To Our Beloved Pets

Books: {Fiction}
Mystery, Indiana
Human Sawdust
The Ghost In My Head
A Righteous Cop

Stories: {Long fiction, novellas}
Mystery, Indiana
The Mind of Luther Biggs
LUTHER

Jenny
Lester Talbot and His Magic Eye
Beautiful Ghosts
Pretty Flamingo
Jack and Norma Jean
The Things We Leave Behind – Volumes 1 – 3
Ghosts of Summer
Gardens
Claustrophobia
The Cemetery Artist
Brain Pie
Beast
The Jailhouse Movie Star
Easy Pickings
The Dominant Thumb
Joyride
The Maverick
Freak
Grandma's Gooseberry Pie
Dancing With the King
Always In My Heart
Hillbilly Moonshine Zombies
Home
Sheva
A Debt Repaid In Full
The Enlightening Darkness
The Good Neighbor
Wander
The Hungry Ones
A Gunfighter's Legacy
Dead Man's Hand
Inhuman Experiments – Part 1, 2, and 3
Jennifer

Spider Bait
Goodnight, My Love
Poor Larry
Creepy Crawl
The Ballad Of Georgie

Other recent book releases by David Boyer
{Now available on Lulu.com}

Dolores Oliver, fondly nick-named 'Lert' by her friends as a term of endearment, was out an out-going and friendly woman who was well liked by all who knew her.

Yet, on September 7, 1974, while on a visit to a local bar to chat with friends, she simply vanished without a trace. Foul play was immediately suspected by her family, who knew in their hearts that they could think of absolutely no one who would want to do her any harm.

Yet her lifeless body was found at the end of October in a bean field by a farmer in Illinois. Lawrence County coroner Dale Nichols was able to make a positive ID through dental records and a ring Mrs Oliver was wearing.

Who would have done such a thing, and why? Hopefully, VANISHED IN VINCENNES will help to finally solve one of the oldest cold cases in Indiana, and bring her family some closure they have sought for so long.

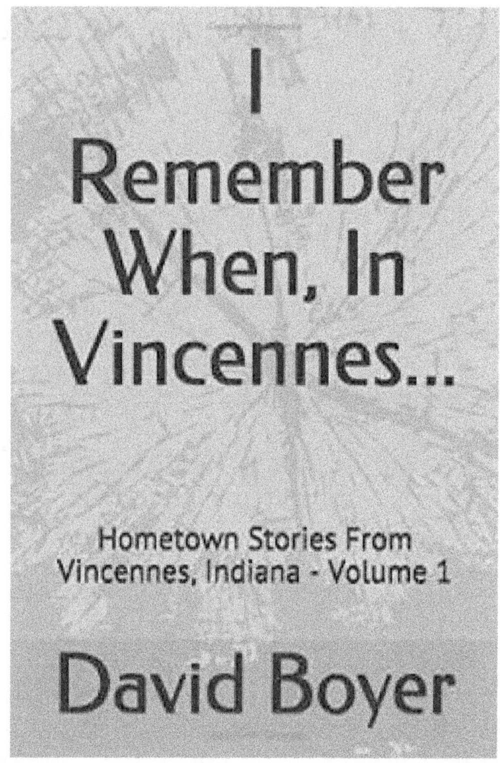

Unfortunately, even small towns – Vincennes included – eventually change, sometimes for the better, and other times, not so much. It's the natural order of things.

Trees grow old and fall. Sidewalks split and crack and are replaced for public safety's sake. Old houses – and all the memories associated with them – are demolished and replaced with parking lots or duplexes. Even historical landmarks, Mother Nature and Father Time having taken their toll, sadly, vanish – except for our own pictures and memories of them.

Luckily for Vincennes residents, local historian Norbert Brown has created a Facebook group page entitled, *Vincennes Remember When*, to help all of us keep our fond memories intact, and to reminisce and enjoy them 24-7.

It was his infinite wisdom of our local history and group page that was the inspiration for this book – and the stories within. Some of these stories may elicit a tear, some laughter.

Some may remind you of an old friend you haven't seen since high school – or, sadly, one that has passed in recent years. Some may remind you of your childhood, your teenage years – or having to bid them farewell, in order to move on to bigger and better things; marriage, children, grandchildren, and a lifetime of wonderful memories that only a tight-knit, loving family can provide.

It is my sincere belief that there will be a story for *everybody* within these pages, regardless of whether you may be a Vincennes history buff or not.

As of 2015, it is believed that there are at least 200 serial killers active in the United States at any given time.

33 of them were from Indiana.

Nobody in their own home town would have wanted to imagine a fledgling {or full fledged} serial killer lurking about, searching for his next victim. Or imagine one being their next door neighbor or the relative of a friend or even attending the local college.

Yet, since the early 1970s, Vincennes, Indiana, Knox County, and Indiana in general has had it's share of cold blooded murder.

It's really sad – as well as terrifying – to even imagine all these brutal, cold blooded murders have taken place in small town communities, where, at one time, we could all trust just about everyone we met at least to the extent they'd do us no harm; a time when could leave our doors unlocked at night or a window open for a cool breeze or not have to worry about where our children were – or if they'd ever come home again.

In SMALL TOWN MURDER, we will be examining local cases, old cases, more recent cases, and the aftermath it leaves behind for the victim's families – as well as taking an in-depth look into a deep, dark, world none of us would ever want to see – but has been here all along, and, most likely, always will be.

Bonus:
Excerpts from the book
Taxi Land
By David Boyer

I was forty two years old when I began driving a taxi.

I had taken early retirement from the military, and although driving a taxi hadn't originally been a part of my plans for my so called golden years, it ended up that way regardless.

I had always been a dream of mine to buy a car, fix it up, and just drive *everywhere*, all over the country, and see things I'd never see in the big city. As it turned out, though, the farthest I'd driven was to the next county over.

But, I was making some extra cash, enjoying driving around, meeting new people, and even making a new friend here and there.

But, believe me, driving a taxi – especially at night – can also be very dangerous.

#

One would think that driving a taxi at night would be excting and interesting, which it could be, yes. But driving a taxi, you don't always know exactly who might call for a ride.

For example, you have your drunks who, while observing a much safer way to get home instead of drving while intoxicated, can still be loud, obnoxious, and even downright mean.

Another example of your average taxi never knowing who {or what} he might run into next, is the night I picked up Billy Hankins.

Billy was a young fella from the North end of

town, who was doing weekends at the county jail as opposed to doing straight time.

In the North end of town, drugs, alcohol, burglary, arson, street fighting, and bar brawling was the norm on any given day. Residents were in fear of their safety after dark – and at times even during the daytime hours. In the North end you either belonged or you didn't and if you didn't, you didn't come in less you got your ass whipped.

Street toughs ruled their corner of the block, and dared any "outsider" to cross their turf. A trip to the store for a loaf of bread was considered an act of bravery.

But somehow, Billy had come out of this hell hole smelling like a rose compared to some of his old buddies, and was even planning on studying for his GED diploma in the near future.

That is, if he could manage not to screw it up.

That night, as I picked him up to deliver him to the county jail, he seemed sort of nervous, fidgety, and didn't have nuch to say. Considering where he was going, I didn't blame him.

As we pulled away from his apartment building, I could see through my rearview mirror that he kept fidgeting with something behind his back and making strange, moaning sounds, as though he was in pain.

Coming to a stoplight ahead, I said, "Are you alright, Billy boy? You seem as nervous as a whore in Church."

He forced a smile and said, "It's cool, Milo. I got some lower back pain, that's all."

I said, "I got some aspirin in the glove box."

He said, "No thanks, I'll be fine."

I said, "Back trouble is a bitch. Take it from me. Are you sure?"

He said, adamantly, "I said, *no*, but thanks."

The light changed and off we went. About two blocks up the street, he started moving around back there again, and making that weird moaning sound. I glanced up in my mirror to see his face was now literally contorted into a rictus of pain and agony, his right hand behind his back.

I pulled over, placed the gearshift in park, leaned over the back seat, and said, "Billy, what in the hell *are* you doing back there?"

His forehead bathed in sweat, he said, "Like I told you, old school, don't worry about it."

I said, "When you ride in *my* cab, I have to worry about it. I'll be legally liable for anything that happens to you."

With his right hand still behind his back, he said, "I said, don't *worry* about it."

I said, "Billy, I may be old school, but I'm not stupid. I know you young punks sneak shit into the jail. Now, what are you up to?"

Billy exposed his right hand to me. He was holding a very small piece of thin plastic, like a piece of a sandwich bag, filled with what looked like tobacco.

I said, "Yeah, so?"

His face flushed, he said, "I'm sneaking this in, if you must know."

I said, "Okay, but why is sneaking that into the jail so painful for you?"

He said, embarrassingly, "I'm trying to cram it up my ass."

I said, "Say what?! Are you nuts?"

He said, "They always check your pockets when you log in, and this way, they won't find it."

Shaking my head in disbelief, I said, "Billy boy, have you ever heard of a strip search? Or a cavity search?"

He said, "I know that, Milo. But I need my tobacco, I really do. I mean, what would you do?"

Lighting a cigarette, I said, "I sure wouldn't be cramming tobacco up my ass, that's for sure."

He said, jokingly, "No, you'd be cramming a can of beer up your ass, right?"

I couldn't argue with that. I said, "Okay, Billy boy. But do me a favor. Just get it done. My own ass is starting to hurt just thinking about it."

With that, off we went again, toward the county jail.

A few minutes later, with his tobacco stash now tucked away firmly up his behind, we pulled up to the jail parking lot. As he climbed out, he said, "I owe you one, Milo. I'll pay you on Friday. Cool?"

I said, "Sure, kid. I know the drill."

As he walked away, I couldn't help but be reminded of my own youth, and the stupid shit I used to do, too.

Except for cramming foreign objects up my butt, that is.

#

About half an hour later, as I cruised the North end for any other potential customers – folks who were too drunk to walk home from the tavern, druggies too high to find their own ass if it was right in front of them, etc.

- was when I spotted old Miss Edwards, one of the local retirees, slowly pushing her scooter down the street, huffing and puffing and having a hard time.

I immediately pulled over, rolled down my window, and said, "Miss Edwards? You need a hand?"

She looked up at me with those old tired eyes, and said, "Oh, Milo. Thank God."

I said, jokingly, "I see that scooter you took from Walmart has failed you again."

She ssaid, jokingly, "Why don't you just say that a little louder, Milo? I don't think the folks over in the next county heard you."

I put the cab in park, climbed out, and looked the scooter over and said, "It's the battery, Margie. I told you that you needed to recharge it now and then."

She said, "Oh yeah, sure. I'll just push it out to Walmart and ask them to charge it for me."

I said, "Smartass."

She said, "Well? Are you just gonna stand there and giggle like a school boy, or are you gonna help me get this piece of crap home?"

I said, "It would be my pleasure."

#

It wasn't just like that in the North end, either.

It was like that all over town, and all over the country, by the year 2022.

I saw it every night almost, older folks just trying to get by, and more often than not, doing just that, *barely* getting by.

I couldn't blame them for being desperate enough to "borrow" a scooter either. Not that I condoned thievery, mind you, but I didn't condone watching our own government robbing us blind, either.

So, as far as I was concerned, Miss Edwards was now the defacto owner of a brand new Walmart scooter.

9 798822 937223